Peter Pan is a little boy who never wants to grow up. One night he comes to the nursery window and invites the Darling children to his home, in Never Never Land. Here they begin their exciting adventures when they meet Indians and pirates who are led by the evil Captain Hook, Peter's greatest enemy...

British Library Cataloguing in Publication Data
Walt Disney's Peter Pan.
  I. Barrie, J.M.   II. Walt Disney Productions
  823'.914[J]   PZ7
  ISBN 0-7214-1022-7

First edition

© WALT DISNEY PRODUCTIONS MCMLXXXVII

Printed in England

WALT DISNEY'S

Peter Pan

Ladybird Books

Wendy Darling shared a big
nursery room with John and
Michael, her two young brothers.
At bedtime she would tell them
wonderful stories about a faraway
place called Never Never Land,
where a boy called Peter Pan lived.

But Wendy was growing up, and was to have a proper bedroom of her own. "No more stories about Peter Pan after tonight!" sighed little Michael. As he spoke, the children heard a gentle tapping at the nursery window.

It was Peter Pan! He had come to take the children on a flying trip to Never Never Land.

"Fly?" cried Wendy. "We can't fly!"

"Then we'll teach you!" answered Peter with a grin. "Come on in, Tink!" he shouted.

There was a buzzing outside the window, and in flew a tiny fairy. "I'm Peter Pan's best friend," she said proudly. "My name's Tinker Bell. *Ting-a-ling!*"

Peter told the children to shut their eyes and think happy thoughts. Then Tinker Bell sprinkled them with golden pixie dust, and the children suddenly found that they were flying round the nursery, bumping into walls and hitting their heads on the ceiling!

When they found that they could really fly, they left the nursery and flew about over the house.

Then, following a trail of Tinker Bell's golden pixie dust, they were off and away to Never Never Land.

When they arrived in Never Never Land, Peter went to check that all was well on his island. He told Tinker Bell to take the children to meet his friends the Lost Boys.

But Tinker Bell was growing jealous of Wendy. Peter Pan seemed to like this girl too much! So Tinker Bell went to tell the Lost Boys that Peter had ordered them to shoot down a bird with a girl's head.

"It's called the Wendy bird!" she said spitefully.

As the children were flying overhead, the Lost Boys shot poor Wendy out of the sky with stones from their catapults. But Peter Pan came swooping down, just in time to save her from crashing. Tinker Bell was furious.

To punish her, Peter said that Tinker Bell must stay away for eight days. She felt very sorry for herself. *"Ting-a-ling!"* she sniffed miserably.

Peter took Wendy off to do some sightseeing, and John was left in charge of Michael and the Lost Boys. Together, the boys set out on an adventure. Their plan was to capture a band of Indian braves who lived on the island.

Unfortunately their plan didn't work and the Indian braves captured the boys instead and took them back to the Indian village.

Peter Pan had taken Wendy to a
beautiful lagoon to visit the
mermaids who lived there. As they
sat by a rock pool they saw a
rowing boat go past.

"It's Captain Hook!" Peter
hissed, ducking behind a rock.

"He's got Princess Tiger Lily.
She's the daughter of the Indian
chief. We've got to
rescue her! She's
my friend!"

Captain Hook was an evil-hearted pirate, and Peter Pan was his greatest enemy. A long time ago, in a fair fight, Peter had cut off the pirate's left hand. Afterwards, the captain had screwed a horrible steel hook to his wrist.

The missing hand had been eaten by a crocodile. It was such a tasty meal that Mr Crock now followed the pirate ship wherever it went, hoping for a chance to gobble up the rest of Captain Hook! Once, the crocodile had swallowed a clock so now he made a loud *tick-tock* as he moved along.

19

Peter and Wendy climbed up to a high ledge. They saw Captain Hook tying Princess Tiger Lily to a rock near the shore. "If you don't tell me where Peter Pan's secret hiding place is," they heard him snarl at the princess, "I'll leave you here on Skull Rock, and when the tide comes in you will drown!"

The girl shuddered, but answered bravely, "I'll never tell you! Never!"

Peter didn't waste a second. He flew down as swift as an arrow. "You again!" howled the pirate, drawing his sword.

Up and down the rocky cliffs they fought until Captain Hook lost his footing and almost fell into the sea. He just managed to hook onto a rock! Down below he could see Mr Crock, his jaws open wide.

But Mr Smee, the boatman,
managed to save his master and
this made the crocodile very cross.
"Next time!" he muttered to
himself as he tick-tock-ticked away
"I'll have him next time!"

Peter and Wendy rescued Tiger Lily from the rock and took her home. The Indian Big Chief was so grateful to Peter for saving his daughter that all the boys were set free and everyone got ready for a big party. After the dancing, Peter was appointed Deputy Big Chief, and a peace pipe was passed round.

Even little Michael tried a puff, but
it made his eyes water! So they all
went back to Peter's secret cave,
tired out after their adventures.

Captain Hook was furious that Peter had beaten him once again.

"Mr Smee," he growled, "I've just had another idea for getting rid of Peter Pan. First, you must fetch Tinker Bell. I need her help!"

Mr Smee sighed. Captain Hook's ideas for getting rid of Peter Pan were always a flop. But the boatman did as he was told and captured Tinker Bell, who was in a very spiteful mood.

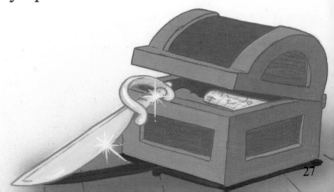

Tinker Bell was delighted when Captain Hook told her that he wanted to capture Wendy and make her into a servant to scrub and cook for the pirates. All the little fairy had to do was to tell him how to find Wendy in Peter Pan's secret hideout.

Tinker Bell dipped her toes in a bottle of ink and danced across a map of Never Never Land, so that her footprints showed the way to Peter's cave. Then the wicked Captain Hook put her in a glass cage and set out to capture Peter Pan.

By now the children were getting homesick. Peter hated the thought of losing all his friends, but he didn't stop them from going.

First, the Lost Boys said farewell and set off to find their own homes again. Then the children turned to Peter Pan, and said goodbye to him. Wendy was the last to leave. "I'll never forget you, Peter!" she said softly.

"You will when you grow up,"
muttered Peter.

"Never!" answered Wendy.

The pirates were all in hiding near Peter's cave, waiting to kidnap the children as they left. First they captured the Lost Boys, then Michael, John and Wendy, and took them off to the pirate ship.

Captain Hook left a parcel on Peter's doorstep, with a label that said: *To Peter from Wendy.*

"This should finish him off!" said the pirate to himself, hurrying away as fast as he could.

But Tinker Bell had seen Captain Hook wrapping the parcel, and she knew that there was a bomb inside. She had guessed that it was meant for Peter Pan.

As the children were taken onto the boat Tinker Bell struggled and kicked inside her glass cage. Suddenly there was a *crack!* and the glass broke. Tinker Bell was free! Forgetting all about her jealousy, away she flew to warn Peter Pan.

The pirates snarled at the children. "Either join the pirate band," they said, "or walk the plank and drown!"

The boys quite liked the idea of being pirates, and forgot all about going home.

But Wendy refused to join up. So
the pirates tied her hands behind
her back, and Captain Hook
pointed to the plank.

"Off you go!" he said. "Walk!"

As Wendy stepped off the end of
the plank, everybody waited for the
splash! as she hit the water. They
waited. And they waited.

But the splash never came! Tinker Bell had reached Peter Pan in time to warn him about the bomb and to tell him where the children were. He had arrived just as Wendy was walking the plank, and had caught her before she fell into the water.

Then Peter Pan fought another duel with Captain Hook. Back and forth they went, the pirate armed with a sword and the brave boy with only his shining dagger.

At last, when they were perched high on a mast, Captain Hook slipped.

"Aaaaagh!" he screamed, as he fell into the sea.

"Dinner time!" thought Mr Crock happily. *"At last!"*

Desperately, the pirate began swimming towards Mr Smee's little rowing boat in the distance.

Mr Crock, ticking for all he was worth, went after him. And the last time the children looked, Mr Crock was catching up!

The Lost Boys set out once again
for home, and this time they
managed to get there safely.

At Peter's command, Tinker Bell
scattered the pirate ship with her
golden pixie dust and the ship
soared high into the air. Soon the
gang plank was stretching out to
touch the nursery windowsill and, in
next to no time, the children were
sound asleep in their own beds.

Next day, the children told their parents all about their adventures in Never Never Land. But the grown ups only shook their heads and smiled. They thought it was just make-believe!

But they were wrong.